# MAREK, THE LITTLE FOOL

## JANINA DOMANSKA

GREENWILLOW BOOKS

NEW YORK

Library of Congress Cataloging in Publication Data
Domanska, Janina.
Marek, the little fool.
Summary: After doing three errands for his family
in his own way, the simple Marek is content to
sit on the stove catching flies all day long.
[1. Folklore–Soviet Union]   I. Title
PZ8.1.D717Mar   [398.2] [E]   81-6966
ISBN 0-688-00912-3          AACR2
ISBN 0-688-00913-1 (lib. bdg.)

TO ELIZABETH SHUB, WITH LOVE

An old couple had three sons. Two were clever, but the third was a simpleton. He was called Marek, the Little Fool. While the two clever brothers grazed the sheep in the field, Marek sat on the stove all day long, catching flies and doing nothing.

One sunny day their mother cooked
a large pot of porridge, and said to
Marek, "Take this to your brothers in
the field. It's almost noon and they will
be hungry."
Marek took the pot and started off.

But when he came out on the road, he suddenly saw his shadow. "Who is this man who walks by my side and won't leave me for a moment?" he thought to himself.

"He probably wants some porridge," Marek decided, and began to throw porridge at his shadow. Before he knew it, he had thrown it all away.

"Eat it, if you are hungry," Marek said angrily. But the shadow continued to walk at his side.

"Oh! What a stupid creature," Marek scolded, and he flung the pot at the shadow. Needless to say, he came to his brothers empty-handed.

"Why have you come?" they asked.
"To bring your dinner."
"Well, where is it?"
"I don't have it. A stranger followed me
all the way here. He was hungry and so
I gave him the porridge and he didn't
even eat it."
"What stranger?" asked the brothers.
"Look, here he is again," said Marek,
pointing to his shadow.

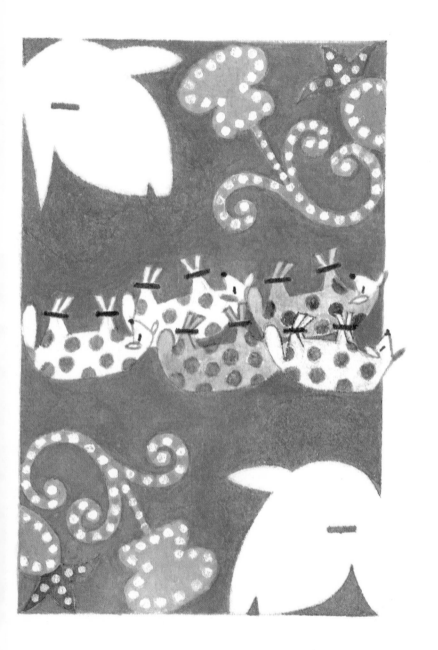

The brothers didn't know whether to laugh or to be angry. At last, they told Marek to tend the sheep while they went to the village to buy some dinner. Marek sat down to watch the sheep. They were scattered all over the field. "This will not do," he thought. He gathered them together, bound their legs, and thought it a job well done.

When the brothers returned and saw
the sheep with their legs bound up,
they were astonished.
"Why did you bind the sheep?" they
asked.
"They wouldn't stay together," Marek
replied. "It was a lot of work for me."
"You are a fool," the brothers said,
and sent Marek home.

Some time passed. It was the day before Easter and the old parents sent Marek to the village to buy the things they needed for the holiday. Marek bought a table, new spoons and cups, pots and pans, and some salt and savory food. He loaded everything on his cart and started to drive home, but his old horse was weak and walked very slowly under the heavy load.

Marek thought to himself, "The table has four legs just like the horse. It can find its own way home." He placed the table on the road and continued on. A flock of ravens circled over him, fighting and croaking.

"The little sisters must be hungry, or they wouldn't cry out like that," he thought. He put the savory food out on the road to feed the ravens.

"Eat, little sisters, eat," he called and traveled on.

Along the road Marek saw a grove of burned trees, black and bare. "Poor things," he thought. "They stand there without any covering. The rain will wet their heads." And he quickly covered them with the pots and pans he had bought, and drove on.

The road home soon took him past a river.

"My poor horse is tired. I will stop so that he can drink," thought Marek. But the horse wasn't thirsty.

"He won't drink because there's no salt in the water," Marek said to himself, and he poured the sack of salt into the river. Still the horse would not drink.

"Why don't you want to drink?" Marek cried. "I poured out a full sack of salt for nothing!"

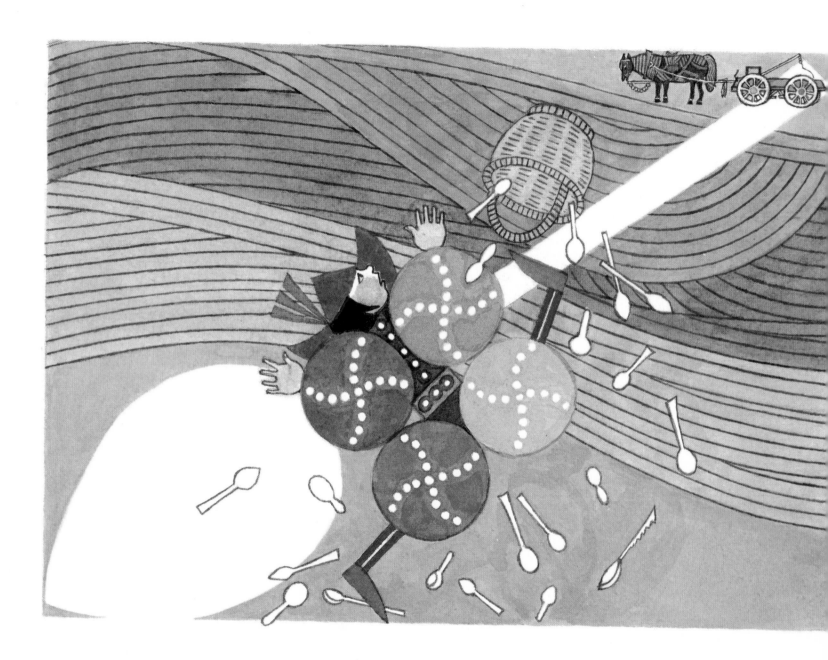

Marek was so angry he left the horse and cart where they were, and taking the basket of spoons which was all he had left, he walked on.

The spoons rattled, *tak-tak-tak-tak-tak*, and Marek thought they were saying, "Marek's a fool, Marek's a fool." He threw the basket down, kicked at it, and said, "Nasty spoons! How dare you make fun of me!"

When he got home, he said, "I'm tired, but I did all the shopping."

"Thank you, Marek, but where is everything?"

"The table is walking home, but undoubtedly it stopped to have a rest. The ravens, sweet sisters, were hungry, and I scattered the food on the road so they might have something to eat. The pots and pans I put on the tree trunks in the grove to keep them dry when it rains.

"The salt I threw into the river because the horse doesn't like sweet water. The spoons made fun of me, so I threw them away."

"What have you done! What have you done!" everyone cried. "Go back and gather everything up."

But only the pots and pans were still where Marek had left them. He knocked out their bottoms, and strung them on a string, to carry them home more easily.

From then on no one asked Marek to do any errands. He sat on the stove catching flies the day long and was very pleased with himself.